The Clumsies

make a

mess of the zoo

First published in paperback in Great Britain by
HarperCollins *Children's Books* in 2011
HarperCollins Children's Books is a division of
HarperCollins*Publishers* Ltd
77–85 Fulham Palace Road, Hammersmith, London W6 8JB

Visit us on the web at www.harpercollins.co.uk

1

Text copyright © Sorrel Anderson 2011
Illustrations copyright © Nicola Slater 2011

ISBN: 978-0-00-733937-2

Printed and bound in England by Clays Ltd, St Ives plc

Mixed Sources
Product group from well-managed
forests and other controlled sources
www.fsc.org Cert no. SW-COC-001806
© 1996 Forest Stewardship Council

FSC is a non-profit international organisation established to promote the
responsible management of the world's forests. Products carrying the FSC
label are independently certified to assure consumers that they come
from forests that are managed to meet the social, economic and
ecological needs of present and future generations.

Find out more about HarperCollins and the environment at
www.harpercollins.co.uk/green

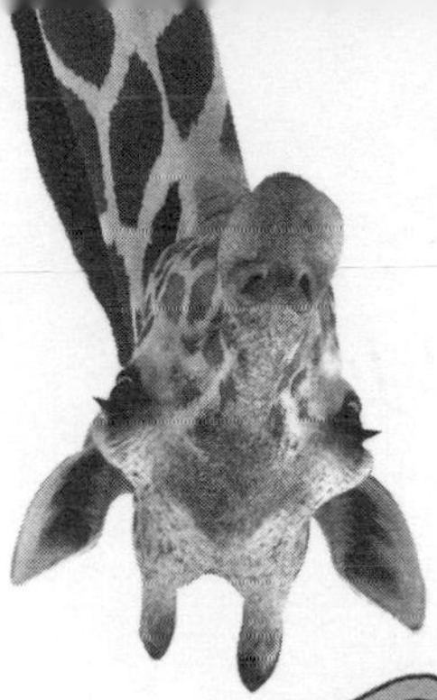

BY SORREL ANDERSON

813072

The Clumsies

make a

mess of the zoo

Illustrated by Nicola Slater

HarperCollins *Children's Books*

For Carol, Freda and Jane

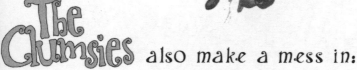 also make a mess in:

The Clumsies Make a Mess

The Clumsies Make a Mess Of
the Seaside

The Clumsies Make a Mess Of
the Big Show

Contents

Nervous
Exhaustion

It was a Tuesday morning and everyone in the office was feeling cheerful. Howard was **humming** a tune and reading a magazine. Purvis and Mickey Thompson were playing a game and eating crisps. And Ortrud the very small elephant was frolicking, knocking things over.

'LOOK OUT, HOWARD,'

shouted Purvis, as Ortrud

crashed into the coat-stand.

'**Oof,**' said
Howard, as the
coat-stand narrowly
missed him.

'That was close,' said Mickey
Thompson.

'It's ever so nice when Mr Bullerton's away, isn't it, Howard?'

'Yes,' said Howard. 'Ever so.'

'How long do you think he'll be gone?' asked Purvis.

'Who can tell?' said Howard. 'I heard he's been told by his doctor to have a long rest. He's suffering from **Nervous Exhaustion.**'

Purvis gasped and Mickey Thompson dropped his bag of crisps.

'Quite,' said Howard.

11

'Are you sure?' asked Purvis.

'I have it on good authority,' said Howard.

'Gosh,' said Mickey Thompson. '**Nervous Exhaustion**, eh?'

'Bit of a **shock**, isn't it?' said Howard, flicking through his magazine.

'**Yes,**' chorused the mice.

'I wouldn't have thought it, would you?' said Howard.

'**No,**' chorused the mice.

Howard resumed his humming and the mice exchanged glances. Mickey Thompson r**aise**d an eyebrow at Purvis, and Purvis shrugged. Mickey Thompson prodded Purvis, and Purvis **coughed**.

'Er, Howard?' said Purvis.

'Mmm?' said Howard.

'What's **Nervous Exhaustion?**'

'Hazard a wild guess,' said Howard.

'Feeling nervous?' hazarded Purvis.

'And?' said Howard.

'Exhausted,' said Purvis.

'Exactly,' said Howard.

Mickey Thompson selected a crisp and ate it, *worriedly*.

'So what you're saying,' he said, 'is he's SpOOked and poopeɑ.'

'If you must,' said Howard.

'Poop poopeɑy poopeɑ', said Mickey Thompson, loudly, and Ortrud started trumpeting.

14

'Enough,' said Howard.

'But it isn't like him,' said Purvis. 'Mr Bullerton's normally so... so...'

'**BOSSY,**' said Mickey Thompson.

'Yes,' said Howard, 'and...'

'**Shouty,**' said Purvis.

'Yes,' said Howard, 'and...'

'S t o m p y,' said Mickey Thompson.

'Yes,' said Howard, 'and...'

'**Angry,**' said Purvis.

15

Howard **thumped** the
magazine down on the desk.

'And,' he
said.

'And what, Howard?' asked
Purvis.

'And now I can't remember
what I wanted to say,' said
Howard.

'He's getting forgetful,'
muttered Mickey Thompson, to
Purvis.

'What?' said Howard.

'It's a symptom,' said Mickey Thompson.

'What is?' said Howard.

'Forgetfulness,' said Mickey Thompson, cheerfully. 'You're growing elderly.'

'WHAT!'

shouted Howard.

'We were discussing Mr Bullerton,' explained Purvis.

'I know we were,' said Howard. 'I am well aware of that, thank you very much, and I am NOT forgetful.'

'Of course not, Howard,' said
Purvis.

'I'm a young man in the
prime of life,' said Howard.

'Yes, Howard,' said Purvis,
rummaging for tea bags. 'But
what do you think caused it?
The Nervous Exhaustion,
I mean.'

'I don't know,' said Howard,
'but I expect I shall get the
blame, as usual.'

'Maybe we should make him a
get well card,' suggested Mickey
Thompson.

'Maybe we shouldn't,' said

18

Howard. 'I've been given strict instructions to leave him alone, in peace and quiet.'

Purvis handed Howard a cup of tea, and Howard brightened.

'And I'll tell you what,' he continued. 'While Mr Bullerton's away, I intend to enjoy some peace and quiet of my own.'

'TRUMPET!'

trumpet**ed** Ortrud,
crashing into a rubber plant.

'Tut,' said Howard,
as the rubber plant narrowly
missed him. 'What's wrong with

Ortrud? Why's she hurtling?'

'I'm not sure,' said Purvis. 'Why are you hurtling, Ortrud?'

Ortrud tooted, and hurtled faster.

'LOOK OUT, HOW— Whoops, too late,' said Mickey Thompson, as Ortrud smashed into a cupboard, and the cupboard landed on Howard.

'Harrumph,' said Howard, extricating himself. 'What this elephant needs is fresh air and exercise.'

'Shall I open the window?' offered Purvis.

'That won't be nearly airy enough for this situation,' said Howard, taking a gulp of tea. 'I think we'd better take the day off and go out somewhere.'

'HURRAY!' cheered Mickey Thompson, bouncing.

22

'Where shall we go?' said
Purvis, **h^opping**.
'Where? Where?'
   'Where do you fancy?'
said Howard.
   'Seaside?' suggested Purvis.
'Too salty,' said Howard.
   'Countryside?' suggested
Purvis.
   'Too muddy,' said Howard.
   'A woodland walk?' suggested
Purvis.
   'Too woody,' said Howard.
   'Ooh. Ooh,' said Mickey
Thompson, waving his hand in
the air.

'Yes, Mickey Thompson?' said Howard.

'CRISP FACTORY,' shouted

Mickey Thompson.

'Too… What do you mean, *crisp factory*?' said Howard.

'They conduct guided tours, and provide free samples. It says so, here,' said Mickey Thompson, *jabbing* the back of his crisp packet.

'No,' said Howard.

'But, Howard,' said Mickey Thompson.

'No crisp factories,' said Howard.

Mickey Thompson sighed, and ate another crisp, dejectedly.

'I wonder what Ortrud would like to do,' said Purvis. Everyone looked at Ortrud, as she started on another circuit of the room.

'It's difficult to tell,' said Howard.

'If only we could speak elephant,' said Mickey Thompson.

25

'THAT'S IT!' **shouted** Purvis, leaping up. 'I'VE GOT IT!'

He **shot** under the desk and shot back out again clutching a green leaflet, decorated all over with pictures of happy-looking animals. 'This is where we should go,' he said, flapping it. 'The **ZOO**!'

'T O O T !'

trumpeted Ortrud.

'HURRAY!' cheered
Mickey Thompson.

'Too many animals,' said
Howard.

The mice gasped, and Ortrud
skidded to a halt.

'But you like animals,
Howard,' said Purvis.

'Yes, Howard,' said Mickey
Thompson. 'Animals are *lovely*.'
He batted his eyelashes at
Howard, energetically.

'One can go off a thing, you know,' said Howard.

'But, Howard,' said Purvis, looking a little upset.

'Oh, go on then,' said Howard. 'The **ZOO** it is.'

'**TOOT!**' trumpeted Ortrud, '**HURRAY!**' cheered Mickey Thompson.

'There'll be other elephants there, you see,' explained Purvis. 'I was thinking it might be good for Ortrud to meet them.'

28

'It certainly can't do any harm,' agreed Howard.

'Off we go, then,' said Mickey Thompson, **rushing** towards the door.

'Wait!' said Purvis.

'What?' said Mickey Thompson.

'We need to prepare,' said Purvis.

'Eh?' said Mickey Thompson.

'For the outing,' said Purvis.

'He's right,' said Howard, putting

the kettle on.'

'There's no sense in **rushing** these things. How long do we need?'

'Around **fifteen** minutes should do it,' said Purvis. 'Certainly no more than **twenty**'

'Perfect,' said Howard. 'We'll set off in **twenty** minutes.'

So everyone **BUSTLED** about preparing for the outing.

Howard made and drank three cups of tea,

to keep him going, he said.
Mickey Thompson put on a pith
helmet and ate some more
crisps. Purvis found a rucksack
and zipped the zoo leaflet into
it. And Ortrud completed seven
circuits of the room,

CRASHED into a chair and **flomped** down in the middle of the floor, panting *heavily*.

'Oh dear,' said Purvis.
'**Nervous Exhaustion**,' said Mickey
Thompson, sounding
knowledgeable.

'I wouldn't be at all
surprised,' said Howard.

'Ortrud, hup!' coaxed Mickey
Thompson. *Hup!*

'She won't budge,' said
Purvis. 'Can you carry her,
Howard?'

'If I must,' sighed Howard,
hoisting her up. Ortud
trumpeted, complainingly,
and went floppy.

'She's *heavy*,' puffed Howard.

'We'll stop from time to
time, for rests,' said Purvis.

'And conspicuous,' grumbled
Howard. 'I don't want to attract
attention.'

'Why's that then?' asked
Mickey Thompson.

'Because strictly speaking I
should be working hard at my
desk,' said Howard, 'not visiting
ZOO s.'

'I see,' said Purvis.

Mickey Thompson pointed at
Howard's mac, **tangled** in
the coat-stand.

'That old mac,' he said. 'We
can use it.'

'My smart mac,' corrected
Howard. 'How?'

'As a disguise,' said Mickey
Thompson. 'If we drape it over

Ortrud, it'll look like you're just carrying a bundle of any old something or other. No one will pay any attention at all.'

'A **trumpeting**, elephant-shaped bundle of any old something or other,' grumbled Howard, as he helped the mice

drape the mac over Ortrud.

'There,' said Purvis. 'That looks almost completely inconspicuous.'

'Tremendous,' said Howard, heading towards the door. 'Now let's get going.'

'Wait!' said Purvis.

'What?' said Howard.

'Take your jacket off,' said Purvis.

'Certainly not,' said Howard. 'I've already given up my mac, and it's starting to rain.'

'I know,' said Purvis.

'Well, then,' said Howard.

'But listen,' said Purvis. 'Just imagine.'

'What am I supposed to be imagining?' said Howard.

'Just imagine,' said Purvis, **dramatically**, 'someone comes into this room.'

'Your point being?' said Howard.

'You're supposed to be here, but you've G O N E, ' said Purvis. 'To the **ZOO**! Word gets back to Mr Bullerton, on his sick-bed, and it tips him over the edge, and he takes a turn for the worse and YOU are in **BIG TROUBLE.**'

'Hmm,' said Howard.

'How would they know about the **ZOO**?' asked Mickey Thompson.

'It doesn't matter about the **ZOO** as such,' said Purvis. 'The point is, he's not here.'

'You said they knew about the **ZOO**,' said Mickey Thompson, and there was a small scuffle.

'Stop that,' said Howard.

'So anyway,' continued Purvis, 'if we hang your jacket on the back of your chair, people will assume you're still somewhere here in the building.'

'Why will they?' asked Mickey Thompson.

'Because it's pouring with rain,' said Purvis. '"He can't be far away from his hardworking desk," is what they'll think. "Only a fool would go out in this without a jacket on." '

'Exactly,' said Howard. 'What do you take me for?'

'But, Howard,' said Purvis. 'You don't want to risk getting into trouble, do you? This way, you're covered.'

'Yes, in water,' muttered Howard, as he took his jacket off and hung it over the back of the chair.

'There,' he said. 'Happy now?'

'I'm not sure,' said Purvis. He studied the jacket, *worriedly*. 'Do you think it'll be enough?'

'We could **plump** it out a bit,' suggested Mickey Thompson.

'How do you mean?' asked Purvis.

'Stuff something into it, and sit it on the chair,' said Mickey Thompson. 'Then it would look like an actual Howard.'

'No it would not,' said Howard, *crossly*.

'We'd need some trousers,' said Purvis, looking at Howard's trousers, *speculatively*.

'If you think I'm going to the

with no trousers on you've got
another think coming,' said
Howard.

'You're probably right,' said
Purvis. 'And even if we made it
look really good, what if
someone spoke to it? When it
didn't speak back it would
arouse suspicion.'

'How about some crisps?'
suggested Mickey Thompson.

'You've had enough crisps for
one morning,' said Howard.

'No, I mean open a bag and put it on the desk,' said Mickey Thompson. 'You wouldn't have left the building in the middle of eating a bag of crisps.'

'Good point,' said Purvis. So they opened a bag of crisps and positioned them **carefully** on Howard's desk.

Then they opened a packet of
biscuits, and a carton of juice,
and a packet of mints, and
another bag of crisps, and
positioned those too.

'That's enough now,' said
Howard.

'It's a pity there's no cake,'
said Mickey Thompson, through
a mouthful of biscuit.

'Come along, come along,' said
Howard, 'and let's attempt to
leave the building as quickly, and
as quietly, and as inconspicuously
as we can, can we?'

'OK,' said the mice.

'OK,' said Howard.

'Let's go,' said the mice.

'Let's go,' said Howard, and
they all rushed out of the room
and down the corridor to the
lift as quickly and quietly and
inconspicuously as they could.

'PING,'

went
the
lift
doors,

opening, and they all rushed in.

'We're going to the

ZOO!'

announced Mickey Thompson,
to the lift.

'Shush,' *hissed* Howard.

'Very nice too,' said the lift, as

it

whooshed them downwards.

'That's a funny-shaped bundle he's got there.'

'Er, mmm,' said Purvis, nervously.

'What's it saying?' said Howard. 'It's saying something, isn't it?'

'No. Nothing,' said Purvis, and Ortrud trumpet**ed**.

'Ooh, it's the little elephant!' said the lift. 'I wondered what it was. What's he got her all wrapped up for? She isn't ill, is she?'

'No,' said Purvis.

'Yes,' said Mickey Thompson.

'Which?' said the lift.

'Neither,' said Purvis.

'Both,' said Mickey
Thompson.

'PING,'
went
the
lift

landing with a **bump**. The

doors flew open and they all

r u s h e d out.

'Wait!' called the lift.
'I'LL EXPLAIN
LATER,' shouted
Purvis, as they ran across the
foyer.

'SHUSH,' shouted
Howard. 'QUIETLY, I SAID.'

'Oops,' said Purvis, as they
emerged into the rain. 'I don't
think anyone noticed us though,
do you?'

'We can only hope,' puffed
Howard. 'Quick, here comes
the bus.' So they all splashed
over to the bus stop and
clambered on to the bus.

'**ZOO**

please,' said Howard, to the

driver.

'Zoo!' said the driver, cheerfully. 'Wet day for it. Which?'

'Yes, er,' said Howard, '**ZOO**, please.'

'No point carrying it,' *giggled* the driver, nodding at Howard's mac. 'Not in this rain. Which'll it be?'

'Er, **ZOO**, please,' said Howard.

'I know,' said the driver. 'Which one?'

'How many are there?' said Howard.

'Two,' said the driver. 'Zoo World, World of Zoo. Which do you want?'

'Zoo World,' *whispered* Purvis, tugging Howard's trouser leg.

'World of Zoo,' *whispered* Mickey Thompson, **t u g g i n g** Howard's other trouser leg.

'Stop **p u l l i n g** my trousers,' *hissed* Howard.

'You what?' said the driver, slightly less cheerfully.

'HURRY UP, CAN'T YOU?'

shouted someone from the queue building up behind.

'Which one do you recommend?' Howard asked the driver.

'Not for me to say,' said the driver, looking enigmatic.

'Which is nearest?' said Howard.

'World of Zoo,' said the driver.

'That one, then,' said Howard.

'Zoo World's bigger,' said the driver.

'That one, then,' said Howard.

'On the other hand…' said the driver.

'GET A MOVE ON!' **shouted** someone else from behind.

'Tell you what,' said the driver. 'I'll surprise you.'

'You do that,' said Howard, paying, and grabbing a ticket.

He hurried to the back of the bus and plunked down , wetly, with the bundle of Ortrud on one knee and Purvis and Mickey Thompson on the other. Everyone started steaming gently as the bus lurched off.

THEY BUMPED DOWN ROADS AND AROUND CORNERS AND DOWN OTHER ROADS

AND AROUND DIFFERENT CORNERS AND AFTER WHAT SEEMED LIKE QUITE A LONG TIME the bus lurched to a halt.

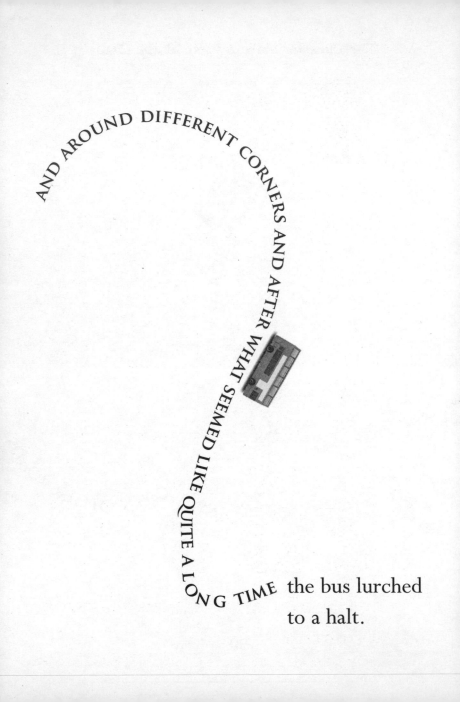

'  ,

shouted the driver, so
Howard s c o o p e d u p
Ortrud and the mice and started

staggering

up the aisle.

'  ,

shouted the driver again,

'  -OOO!'

Everyone on the bus turned to look
at Howard.

'I'm coming, I'm coming,' muttered Howard, staggering to the door and down the steps and out onto the road where, sure enough, there was a **large** green gate with a **large** green sign saying

' **ZOO** '

in **big** red letters.
'At last,' said Howard.

'But I wonder which one it is?' said Purvis.

'Only one way to find out,'
said Howard, going in.
   '**Wow**,' **breathed** Mickey
Thompson, gazing around.

   'Oh no,' gasped Purvis,
staring straight ahead.
   'What?' said Howard.

'It can't be,' said Purvis. 'Can it?'

'What?' said Howard.

'It isn't,' said Purvis. 'Is it?'

'What? What?' said Howard.

'It is,' said Purvis, pointing. 'Over there. It's…'

'MR BULLERTON!' **shouted** Mickey Thompson.

Welcome to the ZOO!

'**Y**IKES!' squawked Howard, diving behind a nearby bush. Ortrud trumpeted in surprise.

'**Yr squshn ush, Hrwd,**' said Mickey Thompson, **muffledly**.

'Sorry,' grunted Howard, rolling off them. 'But what's Mr Bullerton doing here? He isn't supposed to be here.'

'Neither are you,' *whispered* Purvis. 'Strictly speaking.'

'Quite,' *whispered* Howard, 'and if he sees me, I'm for it.'

'Maybe it wasn't really him,' *whispered* Mickey Thompson.

'It really looked like him,' *whispered* Purvis.

'Maybe it was someone

who really looked like him, but wasn't actually him,' *whispered* Mickey Thompson.

'Of course it was him,' *whispered* Howard. 'Who else could it be?'

'Yes, he is distinctive,' agreed Purvis.

'But quite far away,' *whispered* Mickey Thompson. 'We might have been mistaken.'

'Check,' *whispered* Howard. 'We need to be sure.'

So Purvis peeped over the top
of the bush and checked.

'He's gone,' he said.
'GONE?' squawked
Howard. 'What do you mean,
gone?'

'Moved off,' said Purvis. 'Disappeared.'

Howard spun about, frantically.

'But this is worse,' he said. 'He might loom up at any moment.'

'What do you think we should do?' asked Purvis.

'Leave,' said Howard. *Fast.*

'But, Howard,' chorused the mice, **disappointedly**.

71

'You said we could have a day out at the **ZOO**, Howard,' said Mickey Thompson.

'Yes, I know I did,' said Howard, 'but—'

'And Ortrud wants to meet the other elephants, Howard,' said Purvis.

'Yes, I know she does,' said Howard, 'but—'

'It's important for her **Nervous Exhaustion**, Howard,' said Mickey Thompson, giving Ortrud a nudge. Ortrud tooted, plaintively.

'Yes, yes, all right,' said
Howard. 'Just let me think.'

'We could go to the other
ZOO instead,' suggested
Purvis.

'We don't know the way,' said
Howard.

73

'We could ask,' said Purvis.

'By "*we*" I take it you mean
"*I*",' said Howard.

'Well, yes,' said Purvis. 'I
happened to notice an
INFORMATION POINT
when I was looking for
Mr Bullerton. You could try
there.'

Howard sighed and peeped,
carefully, over the top of the
bush. Purvis was right: some
way off, in the middle of a patch
of concrete, sat a little wooden
hut marked **INFORMATION
POINT**.

'It's too risky, Purvis,' said Howard, crouching down again. 'That hut's very exposed. If Mr Bullerton comes back while I'm there he'll see me for sure.'

'But I've got an idea,' said Purvis.

'So have I,' said Howard. 'We'll go back to the office and come another day.'

'No, wait,' said Purvis, pulling leaves off the bush and pushing them into the neck of Howard's shirt.

'Get off!' said Howard, brushing them out. 'What are you doing?'

'CAMOUFLAGING you,' said Purvis, putting them back.

'Here, Howard,' said Mickey Thompson, lunging at Howard's

face with a handful of mud and
smearing it, helpfully.

'*Bleugh!*' said Howard.

'There,' said Purvis, adding some twigs. 'You blend in beautifully. Stay close to the ground and if he sees you at all he'll think you're foliage.'

'Would that I were,' said Howard, through gritted teeth. 'Foliage has an easy life.'

'The coast's clear,' said Purvis, checking.

'All foliage has to do is sit around all day being foliage,' grumbled Howard.

'I should go now if I were you,' said Purvis. 'Before he comes back.'

Muttering crossly, Howard wrenched off a branch of bush, held it aloft and began crawling towards the **INFORMATION POINT**. 'HURRAY!' cheered Mickey Thompson. 'GO ON, HOWARD!'

Howard reversed, quickly.

'Shuuuussshhh!' he *hissed*.

'No. Attracting. Attention.'

'Sorry, Howard,' *whispered* Mickey Thompson.

Howard set off once more, and the Clumsies peeped over the top of the bush and watched.

'He's taking his time,'
observed Mickey Thompson.

'It's because of the mud and
puddles,' said Purvis. 'I expect
he'll go faster on the concrete.'

'Oh,' said Mickey Thompson.
'Oh, look! There are some
people.'

'Mmm,' said Purvis, *worriedly*.

'Do you think they've noticed
him?' asked Mickey Thompson.

'Mmm,' said Purvis,
worriedly. 'We should have
done a better job with the
CAMOUFLAGE.'

'He's gone very still,' said
Mickey Thompson.

'So have the people,' said
Purvis.

'I wonder what's going to
happen next,' said Mickey
Thompson, who was enjoying
himself.

'I can't bear to watch,' said
Purvis, covering his eyes. 'Tell
me.'

'They're moving towards him,' said Mickey Thompson, 'and…oooooh…'

'What?' squeaked Purvis.

'No, it's OK,' said Mickey Thompson. 'They're backing away now. They're running, actually. And they've gone.'

Eventually Howard reached the **INFORMATION POINT** and staggered upright, **stiffly**.

'Anyone in?' he called, **kn^{oc}kⁱng**, and a noise came from inside that sounded like someone blowing an extremely loud raspberry. '*Tthhppf*', it went.

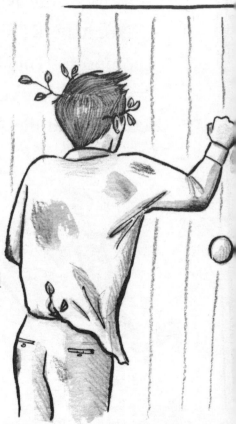

'HELLO?' called Howard, **kn⁰ᶜkⁱng** again, and rattling the handle. The door opened a

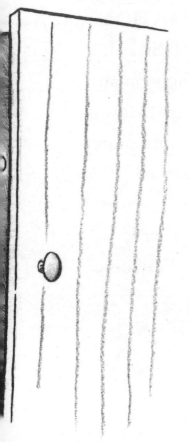

crack and a woman peered out.

'Hello,' *whispered* the woman, glancing around nervously.

The *noise* happened again, and Howard jumped.

'Welcome to

the zoo,' *whispered* the woman.

'Er,' said Howard.

'Yes?' *whispered* the woman.

'Is this the **INFORMATION POINT**?'*whispered* Howard.

'Yes,' *whispered* the woman. She closed the door and Howard waited, and waited some more, then he knocked again and the woman peered out.

'It's you,' she *whispered*, sounding surprised. 'Welcome to the **ZOO**.'

'You've already— *oof*,' said
Howard, staggering
backwards

as the *noise* happened again,
even more loudly, and a
leaflet flew through the door
and hit him in the face.

'Whoops,' *whispered* the
woman. 'It was the wind.'

'Well, really,' said Howard, 'I
don't—'

'Goodbye,' *whispered* the
woman, closing the door, firmly.

'Extraordinary,' muttered
Howard. He crawled quickly
back to the bush and arrived
behind it, **puffing.**

'I'm back,' he **puffed**.

'How did it go?' asked Purvis. 'Did you get the directions?'

'No,' said Howard. 'Some people have no idea how to run an **INFORMATION POINT**.

'What was it that hit you?' asked Mickey Thompson.

'This,' said Howard, chucking the leaflet on to the ground. It was green, and decorated all over with pictures of happy-looking animals.

'It's the same as Purvis's,' said Mickey Thompson. Purvis picked it up and studied it.

'*Welcome to the Zoo!*' he read out.

'Don't you start,' groaned Howard.

'Welcome to the  World zoo or welcome to the World of zoo?' asked Mickey Thompson.

'I could do with a cup of tea,' said Howard, closing his eyes.

'It doesn't specify,' said Purvis, 'but the **ZOO** in this leaflet seems to be a different zoo from the zoo in my leaflet.'

He rummaged in his rucksack, found his leaflet, and studied it.

'It looks the same to me,' said Mickey Thompson. 'What does it say?'

'*Welcome to the Zoo!*' read out Purvis.

'I could definitely do with a cup of tea,' said Howard.

Purvis **carefully** placed the leaflets side by side on the ground and stared at them.

'Hmm,' he said. He turned them over and stared at the backs; then he opened them up and examined the maps in the middle.

'Map of the zoo,' said Mickey
Thompson, **p o i n t i n g** .
'And the same map of the same

,' he said, **p o i n t i n g** at the
other one.

'But, look,' said Purvis. 'In
the leaflet on the left the
**ANIMAL ENCOUNTER
ENCLOSURE** is at number
9 on the map, and in the leaflet
on the right,' he said, tapping it,
'the **ANIMAL
ENCOUNTER**

ENCLOSURE is at
number **10**.'

'It's probably a misprint,' said Howard.

'And here,' said Purvis, tapping again, 'we have **NOCTURNAL CREATURES** at number **37,** while the other number **37**'s an **ICE-CREAM KIOSK**.'

'Let's go there,' said Mickey Thompson, quickly.

'I'm not sure we can,' said Purvis. 'It's been crossed out.'

'WHAT?' said Mickey Thompson.

'There's more,' said Purvis. 'Look again at the pictures of

the animals on the front.'

Howard and Mickey Thompson looked again at the pictures of the animals on the front.

'See?' said Purvis.

'No,' said Howard and Mickey Thompson.

'Anteater, elephant, penguin, unusual thing, monkey, giraffe,' said Purvis, pointing them out.

'But on this one,' he continued, 'it's anteater, elephant, penguin, unusual thing, monkey.

'No giraffe!' **gasped** Mickey
Thompson.

'Exactly,' said Purvis.

'Where's it gone?' *whispered*
Mickey Thompson.

'I don't know,' said Purvis.
'And the elephant looks a lot
less happy in that picture, too.'

Ortrud wriggled out of
her wrapping and hurried over,
tooting.

'Managing to walk now, are
we?' said Howard.

'She's worried about the elephant,' said Purvis.

'And the missing giraffe,' added Mickey Thompson.

'I'm sure there's a simple explanation for it all,' said Howard, yawning, and checking his watch. 'Does either of those leaflets happen to mention a tea room?'

'Let's see,' said Purvis. 'There's **CAFÉ MARMOSET** at number **29**, both leaflets.'

'Right, then,' said Howard.

'And there's the **BLUE LAGOON BISTRO** at number **76**, this leaflet.'

'Fine,' said Howard.

'And there's the **HUT SUT HIP HOP HOT DOG HUT** at number **3** that leaflet.'

'Good heavens,' said Howard. 'And the **SNACK ATTACK SHACK** at number **6** this...'

'Enough,' said Howard. 'I've got a fancy for **CAFÉ MARMOSET**.'

'Number **29** in both leaflets,' said Mickey Thompson, helpfully.

'Which must be a good sign,' said Howard. 'Come along, let's go and find it.'

'But, Howard,' said Purvis. 'I'm not sure it's safe.'

'Eh?' said Howard.

'Mr Bullerton,' said Purvis. **EEK,'** *screeched* Howard. He flung himself flat on his front and covered his head with his arms.

'What's up, Howard?' asked Mickey Thompson, cheerfully.

'Where is he? Has he gone?' gurgled Howard, his face in a puddle.

'No, I didn't mean he's *here* here,' said Purvis. 'I meant he *might* be here. I mean, I know he is here, somewhere, but he *isn't* here right now here. If you see what I mean.'

Howard sat up, **groaning.**

'I'd forgotten about Mr Bullerton,' he said, mopping his face.

'It's because you're getting elderly and forgetful, Howard,' *giggled* Mickey Thompson.

'Quiet, you,' said Howard, still mopping.

'Number **29**'s rather a long way to crawl, you see,' said Purvis, 'and I'm not sure the CAMOUFLAGE is up to it.'

'Oh, I don't know,' said Howard. 'I managed the trip to the **INFORMATION POINT** and back.'

'I think those people might have **spotted** you, though,' said Purvis. 'They looked as though they had.'

'Well, yes, they did,' admitted Howard. 'But they should have minded their own business.'

'Possibly,' said Purvis, 'but—'

'Which is what I told them,' said Howard.

'Yeah, SHOO!' cheered Mickey Thompson, shaking his fist at some imaginary intruders.

'Hmm,' said Purvis, frowning.

'What do you mean, *hmm*,' said Howard.

'You were supposed to be being a bush,' said Purvis. 'A talking bush would attract attention, not the other way around.'

'Well it's too late to worry about that now,' said Howard.

'I think you'd better stay here,' said Purvis, 'and we'll go and see if we can find you some better CAMOUFLAGE.'

'And a take away cup of tea,'

said Howard.

'We'll, see what we can do,' said Purvis.

'Well don't take too long,'
said Howard. 'I can't hide here
all day, you know.'

'Of course not, Howard,' said
Purvis.

'It's most inconvenient,'
grumbled Howard. 'I was
supposed to be enjoying a time
of tranquillity, not rolling
around in the mud dodging
roving Bullertons and nosy
members of the public.'

'We'll be as quick as we
can,' promised Purvis. He
picked up the leaflets, Mickey
Thompson adjusted his pith

110

helmet, and they tip-toed round
the side of the bush and set off
across the zoo. Tooting loudly,
Ortrud trotted after them.

'**Big**, isn't it?' said Mickey Thompson, after they'd been going for a while. '**Even Bigger** than I was expecting,' said Purvis.

'But I thought there'd be
more animals,' said Mickey
Thompson. 'We haven't seen
any yet.'

'What's that over there?' said Purvis, **pointing**.

'A dragon!' said Mickey Thompson.

'Eh?' said Purvis.

'Oh. A rock,' said Mickey Thompson, disappointedly.

'No, behind that,' said Purvis. 'I thought I saw something

They watched.

'Nothing,' sighed Mickey Thompson. 'Pity,' said Purvis, 'but look, there's a sign-post. Maybe that'll help.' They ran over and gazed up at it.

AZURE ZONE: FRUIT BATS; BLACK-CRESTED MACAQUES

'AZURE ZONE: FRUIT BATS; BLACK-CRESTED MACAQUES,'

read out Purvis.

'Which number?' asked Mickey Thompson, and Purvis consulted his leaflets.

'Seven,' he said, 'in both.'

'We're still quite a way from number **29** then,' said Mickey Thompson.

'Mmm,' said Purvis.

'Might there be a short cut?' asked Mickey Thompson.

'Mmm,' said Purvis, still studying the leaflets.

'Mmm yes or mmm no?'
asked Mickey Thompson.

'Mmm I don't know,' said
Purvis. 'But listen: the **HUT
SUT HIP HOP HOT
DOG HUT'S** at number **3**
in one of the leaflets and I don't
remember passing it, do you?'

'No,' said Mickey Thompson. 'And I would definitely have noticed.'

'That's what I thought,' said Purvis, 'so I reckon we're here.' He showed Mickey Thompson the place on one of the leaflets. 'There should be ring-tailed lemurs to the left, and elephants just around—'

'TOOOOOT!' trumpeted Ortrud, racing off.

118

'PURVIS!' shouted
Mickey Thompson.
'ORTRUD!' shouted
Purvis. 'COME BACK!'
   The mice chased Ortrud
down a narrow path, over a
patch of grass and across an
ornamental bridge, but she was
too fast for them.

'We've lost her,' **puffed** Purvis, as they arrived on the other side of the boating lake.

'Bother,' panted Mickey Thompson. 'Isn't it pretty,

though? Look, there are ducks and everything.'

'Yes, it's *lovely*,' said Purvis, gazing about. 'But where is she?'
'I wish I'd brought some bread,' said Mickey Thompson.

'THERE!' **shouted** Purvis. Ortrud's bottom could be seen wiggling through a gap in a nearby fence, so they set off again over the grass and

through the hole and down and around some spiral steps,

fetching up in front of a big metal door marked

"NO ENTRY."

Lower down on the door was a sign saying

"STRICTLY PROHIBITED",

and underneath that was another sign saying

"KEEP OUT! Trespassers will be PROSECUTED!",

and underneath *that* someone had drawn a skull and crossbones with a thick black marker pen and written

"plees go away plees"

Purvis and Mickey Thompson looked at each other and gulped.

'Well, we can't just leave her, can we?' said Purvis.

Mickey Thompson shook his head.

'Come on, then,' said Purvis. Very gently, he pushed at the door and, rather surprisingly, it swung wide open and they found themselves stepping into a **large** room full of beanbags, and cups of tea, and animals.

'There's Ortrud,' said Mickey Thompson, **p o i n t i n g** .

'Yes, but who's that with her?' said Purvis. 'Surely it can't be—'

'ALLEN!' shouted Mickey Thompson.

The Clumsies Make a Mess at the Zoo

Raspberry
Recovery
Part 1

he mice were right, it was
Howard's dog, Allen, perched
on a beanbag, drinking banana
milk through a bendy
straw.

Ortrud was sitting next to him,
with a cup of tea.

'YOO-HOO!'

called Mickey Thompson. All
the animals in the room turned
to look at Mickey Thompson.

'Whoops,' he said, backing
behind Purvis.

Allen put down his milk and
rushed over.

'It's OK,' he said to the animals. 'They're friends of mine.'

'Oh. Hellooo,' chorused the animals, waving.

'Er, hellooo,' chorused Purvis and Mickey Thompson, waving back.

The animals resumed their
activities, and Allen showed the
mice over to his beanbag.

'What a *lovely* surprise,' he
said. 'First Ortrud, and now
you!'

'Yes!' agreed the mice.

'But why are you here?' asked Allen. 'There isn't anything wrong with Howard, is there?'

'No, Howard's fine,' said Purvis.

'Phew,' said Allen.

'Although muddy,' added Mickey Thompson.

'Sorry?' said Allen.

'Because of the CAMOUFLAGE,' explained Mickey Thompson. 'Oh, and he lay in a puddle.'

'Did he?' asked Allen. 'I wonder why.'

'I don't think he meant to,'
said Purvis. 'It just happened to
be behind the bush he's hiding
behind.'

'Bush?' gasped Allen.

'Yes,' said the mice.

'He's not at the office?'
gasped Allen.

'No,' said the mice.

'I don't understand,' said
Allen. 'He set off for work this
morning. Did he fall down on
the way?'

'Not as far as I know,' said
Purvis.

Allen scratched his head. 'Er,

shall I get us some drinks?' he
suggested, 'and then you can
explain from the beginning.'

'Yes, please!' said the mice.

'Banana milk, please,' said
Mickey Thompson, quickly.

'I'd quite like a cup of tea,'

said Purvis. 'And we're
supposed to be taking one back
for Howard, too.

'Back where, though?' asked
Allen. 'If he isn't at work, where
is he?'

'Behind the bush, like we
said,' said Mickey Thompson.

'And the bush is where?' said
Allen.

'Here!' said Purvis. 'At the

'Oh dear,' said Allen.

'We came for a day out, you see,' said Mickey Thompson. 'It was because of all the **Nervous Exhaustion,** really, and Howard said no about the crisp factory so this seemed the next best thing.'

Allen gazed at the mice and the mice smiled back at him, cheerfully. Allen continued

gazing and the mice smiled and
nodded at him, encouragingly.
After a while Mickey Thompson
coughed, and said, 'So, um,
would a little bit of banana milk
be OK, please, Allen? Only I'm
quite thirsty.'

'Of course,' said Allen,
coming to. 'Sorry. Wait here.'
He hurried off to a small
kitchen area and came back

with some banana milk for
Mickey Thompson, another
apple juice for Ortrud, a cup of
tea in a proper cup for Purvis, a

cup of tea in a take-away cup for
Howard, and a maroon-
coloured smoothie for himself.

'It's a "Boysenberry Bonanza",'
he explained to Mickey
Thompson, who was eyeing it. 'I
fancied a change.'

'I'll try one of those next,'
said Mickey Thompson.

'So, Allen,' said Purvis,
sipping his tea and settling on to
the beanbag. 'How come you're
here?'

'I pop down if I feel like some company,' said Allen. 'I know a short cut from home, and it's a pleasant change of scene. The thing is...' He glanced around, nervously. The mice glanced around too.

'What is it, Allen?' asked Purvis.

'The thing is,' *whispered* Allen. 'Howard doesn't know.'

Mickey Thompson gave a loud *slurp* and several animals jumped.

Purvis shushed him.

'I'm not doing anything,' said Mickey Thompson.

'Drink it more quietly,' *hissed* Purvis. 'And slower.'

Mickey Thompson did another *slurp*, and there was a small scuffle.

'Oh dear,' said Allen.

'Sorry, Allen,' said Purvis, settling down again. 'Howard wouldn't mind you coming here, though, would he?'

'I don't know,' said Allen. 'Strictly speaking, I'm supposed to be asleep in my basket, not visiting zoos.'

'I see,' said Purvis.

'Did you leave anything in the basket?' asked Mickey Thompson.

'Um, my blanket was in there,' said Allen, 'and my blue octopus.'

'Does either of them look anything like you?' asked Mickey Thompson.

'The blanket's the same kind of colour,' said Allen. 'But flatter.'

'You should have stuffed something in it,' advised Mickey Thompson.

'Should I?' said Allen.

'In case someone comes looking,' said Mickey Thompson, ominously.

'Oh dear,' said Allen. 'I didn't think. I don't want to get into trouble.'

'Don't worry, Allen,' said Purvis. 'We won't mention any of this to Howard if you don't want us to, although I think he'd understand.'

'I'm not sure I'll be able to come for much longer, anyway,' said Allen, sighing. 'Everything's changing.'

'How do you mean?' asked Purvis.

Allen did more nervous glancing.

'*It's Mr Bullerton*,' he *whispered*.

Mickey Thompson spluttered milk everywhere and started to choke.

'Oo-er,' said a porcupine,
who was sitting nearby. 'I got
splashed.'

'He had a bit of a shock,' explained Purvis, patting and mopping.

'I'm ever so sorry,' said Allen. 'When I said *"It's Mr Bullerton"* I meant—'

'WHERE?'

shrieked the porcupine, leaping up.

'No, nowhere,' said Allen, as several animals hid behind beanbags. 'Well, he's somewhere, I suppose, but—'

Several of the animals squealed.

'But he isn't *here* here, if you see what I mean,' said Allen. 'I was just trying to tell the mice about him and the zoo.'

The animals came out from behind their beanbags, gingerly.

'He's the reason we're hiding in here,' said Allen. 'He's been visiting an awful lot lately, you see.'

'I wonder why,' said Purvis.

'He told the zoo keeper he's doing it to relax,' said Allen, 'but Mr Bullerton's idea of relaxing seems to be picking fights, and making complaints, and trying to take over, and bossing everyone around.'

'Don't forget Raspberry,' said an otter. 'Tell them about Raspberry.'

'Yes, Raspberry,' said the animals. 'Raspberry!' There

were mutterings, and one or
two shouts.

'Raspberry?' said Purvis.

'It was most unfortunate,' said
Allen, sounding upset. 'He got
into a spot of bother over an ice
cream, and—'

'Ice cream?' said
Mickey Thompson.

'Yes,' said Allen,
'it belonged to
Mr Bullerton, and—'

'What kind of an
ice cream?' said
Mickey Thompson.

'Tutti-frutti,'

154

said Allen. 'A **large** one; with strawberry sauce.'

'Ooooh,' breathed Mickey Thompson.

'I know,' agreed Allen. 'Raspberry was only taking an interest, but Mr Bullerton became enraged, and chased him away, and nobody's seen him since.'

'No!' gasped Mickey Thompson.

'Yes,' said Allen.

'Poor Raspberry,' said Mickey Thompson.

'But, Allen,' said Purvis, 'who – or what – is Raspberry?'

'Oh, didn't I say?' said Allen. 'He's a giraffe.'

'Purvis!' squeaked Mickey Thompson, grabbing on to Purvis. Purvis held up the leaflet with the picture of the giraffe on it.

'Is this him?' he asked.

'That's him,' confirmed Allen. 'Isn't he sweet? We've all been so worried, especially Maud.'

'Maud being...?' said Mickey Thompson.

'Oh, didn't I say that either?' said Allen. 'She's——'

'Wait,' said Purvis. He held up the giraffe-free leaflet, and tapped the picture of the less-than-happy elephant.

'Is this her?' he asked.

'That's her,' nodded Allen.

'She looks a lot like Ortrud,' said Mickey Thompson.

'Yes, they're similar,' said

Allen, 'although Ortrud hasn't got Maud's, um…' His words trailed off.

'Maud's, um… what?' asked Mickey Thompson.

'Well, I don't like to be personal,' said Allen, 'but sometimes she can have rather a, um…'

'Rather, a um… what?' asked Mickey Thompson, just as the door crashed open and an elephant appeared.

'IT'S ME!'

boomed the elephant.

'… *loud voice*,' *whispered* Allen, and Ortrud **toot**ed, excitedly.

'Come on,' said Allen. 'I'll introduce you.' He led the mice and Ortrud over to the far end of the room, where there was a **large** piece of paper stuck on the wall with the words

"OPERASHUN RARSBERRY"

written on it.

Huddled underneath it were the
anteater, the penguin, the
monkey, the unusual thing and a
very small elephant that looked
almost, but not exactly, like
Ortrud.

'HELLO,'
boomed
the elephant, extremely loudly,
and Purvis and Mickey
Thompson got blown a little bit
backwards.

'Steady, Maud,' said the
unusual thing.

'STEADY, Maud,' **boomed**
Maud, moderately loudly. 'Meet
Peg, Bob, Jan and
Chrysanthemum,' she said,
gesturing towards the other
animals.

'Hellooo,' chorused Peg, Bob,
Jan and Chrysanthemum, waving.

'Hellooo,' said Mickey Thompson and Purvis, waving back. Ortrud tooted, and waved her trunk.

'So, Maud,' said Purvis. 'Allen tells us you've been having problems with Mr Bullerton.'

'YES,' **boomed** Maud. 'CHRYSANTHEMUM?'

'Yes, Maud?' said the unusual thing.

'Could we have the list, please?' asked Maud, and Chrysanthemum scampered off and scampered back again trailing an enormously long piece of paper made from a lot of normal-sized pieces of paper stuck end to end with sticky tape.

'Shall I read all of it or just the best bits?' *whispered* Chrysanthemum.

'Call them "*edited highlights*",' *whispered* Maud, 'not "*best bits*".'

'Right,' *whispered*
Chrysanthemum.
 'Go on, then,' *whispered* Maud.
 'Err,' *whispered*
Chrysanthemum. 'Ooh.'

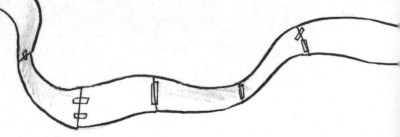

'What's wrong?' *whispered*
Maud.

'I've gone shy,' *whispered*
Chrysanthemum. 'You read it.'

So Maud took it, and
everyone else sat down on the
floor in front of her to listen.

'THE LIST,' she announced. 'B.'

'Eh?' said Allen.

'Very funny,' said Maud.

'Sorry?' said Allen.

'I was about to explain,' explained Maud, 'that I shall be referring to Mr Bullerton as "B" so as to save time and avoid repetition.'

'Good idea,' said Purvis.

'I thought so,' said Maud, 'but I wouldn't wish to confuse you.'

'It's OK, we understand,' said Purvis.

'I'm not sure Allen does,' said Maud.

'I do,' said Allen. 'I do understand, don't I?' he *whispered* to Purvis.

'Of course you do, Allen,' *whispered* Purvis.

'WHISPERING?'

Maud, gazing around.

'Sorry, Maud,' said Purvis.

'SORRY, Maud,' **boomed** Maud.

'Shall I continue?'

'Please do,' said Purvis.

'THE LIST,' announced Maud, again. 'Edited highlights thereof:

'*B* **shouted** *at the* **INFORMATION POINT** *lady and made her cry.*

B **shouted** *at the Zoo Keeper and made him cry.*

B was rude about this zoo and said it is disorganised.

B was unkind about us animals and said that we are lazy.

B made hurtful remarks about Chrysanthemum.

'He said something like me shouldn't be on the leaflet, and no one can tell what I am,' *whispered* Chrysanthemum to Purvis.

'I see,' *whispered* Purvis.

'Can you tell what I am?' *whispered* Chrysanthemum, **worriedly**.

'Of course,' *whispered* Purvis.

'What am I?' *whispered* Chrysanthemum.

'Unusual,' *whispered* Purvis, 'and *lovely*.'

Chrysanthemum looked pleased.
'MORE WHISPERING?'
boomed Maud,
gazing around again.

'Sorry, Maud,' said Purvis.

'SORRY, Maud,' said Maud.

Purvis and Mickey Thompson
exchanged glances, and
shrugged.

'I'll continue,' said Maud,
continuing:

*B made the Zoo Keeper stop our
food.*
*B threw an ice cream at the ice-
cream kiosk man.*

B chased Raspberry and made him disappear.

'See what I mean?' *whispered* Allen, to Purvis.

'Yes,' *whispered* Purvis, back.

'What is it now?' *whispered* Maud, and Purvis jumped.

'I was just telling Allen I saw what he meant about Mr Bullerton causing trouble,' explained Purvis.

'AH!' **boomed** Maud. 'GOOD! So will you help us, please?'

'Of course we will,' said

Purvis.

'WE MUST FIND
RASPBERRY,'

emphasised Maud.

'Raspberry,' muttered the
other animals. 'Raspberry.'

'And we must lose
BULLERTON,' crescendoed
Maud. 'Make him go away.'

'We'll certainly try,' said
Purvis.

'Come on then!' said Maud,
bouncing.

'OK,' said Purvis. 'Well,
first—'

'What are we waiting for?'

bounced Maud. 'What do you think we should do?'

'Well, first—' said Purvis.

'It's been a worrying time, you see,' said Maud, suddenly sighing. 'We've run out of ideas.'

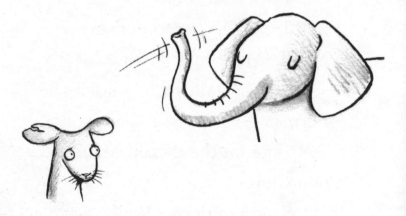

'Right,' said Purvis. 'First, tell us what you've done so far.'

'THIS!' said Maud, pointing at the 'OPERASHUN RARSBErRY' poster, proudly. 'What do you think?'

'It's a good start,' said Purvis.

'Maud drew the outlines,' explained Chrysanthemum, 'and the rest of us coloured them in.'

'Yes, it took ages,' said Allen. 'We wanted to make it look nice.'

'And it does,' said Purvis, 'very, but maybe we should—'

'I did the 'O',' added Chrysanthemum.

'OH!' **shouted** Mickey Thompson.

'Whatever's the matter?' said
Purvis.

'I've only just noticed,' said
Mickey Thompson. 'It's all in
giraffe colours.'

'EXACTLY!'
boomed Maud.

'So, we've got the poster,' said
Purvis. 'Anything else?'

The animals shook their
heads.

'Never mind,'
said Purvis.
'Let's think of
some other
ideas.'

'What kind of ideas?'
asked Chrysanthemum.

'We won't know until we
think of them,' said Purvis, so
everyone thought.

'GOT ONE!'
boomed Maud, almost
immediately. 'We could MAKE
A POSTER.'

'Er,' said Purvis.

'I know what you're thinking,'

said Maud, 'but this one would have **"OPERATION MR BULLERTON"** written on it. THERE!'

'Hmm,' said Purvis.

'In what kind of colours, though?' asked Allen.

'How about blue?' suggested Mickey Thompson. 'He often wears a blue tie.'

'Ooh,' said Chrysanthemum.
'I like blue.'

'So do I!' said Allen. 'Oh,
but… oh dear…'

'What is it, Allen?' asked
Purvis.

'Well,' said Allen, 'if Mr
Bullerton wears a blue tie, he
probably likes blue too, and if
he does, and we make a blue
poster, he might like the poster
so much that he stays here for
ever, so he can carry on seeing
it.'

'Good point, Allen,' said
Mickey Thompson.

'YES!' said Purvis, leaping up. 'And using the same principle we can lure him away.'

Everyone looked at Purvis, blankly.

'Listen,' said Purvis. 'We make an enormous poster advertising something he likes,

with lots of arrows pointing out
of the zoo and far away,

and he'll notice, and he'll follow,
and then… GONE. See?'

'Hurray!' cheered Mickey
Thompson.

'Shall it be blue?' asked
Chrysanthemum.

'If it seems best,' said Purvis.

'Now, we need to think of something he likes.'

'Blue,' said Mickey Thompson. 'We've decided that.'

'Yes, but something more,' said Purvis.

'Pink,' offered Chrysanthemum.

'RED,' boomed Maud. 'GREEN. PURPLE.'

'I meant something that's not a colour,' said Purvis.
'Something to visit, or do.'

'Oh, like a cake sale,' said Mickey Thompson.

'Exactly,' said Purvis.

'Cakes have colours,' objected Maud.

'And Mr Bullerton doesn't like cake,' said Allen, *worriedly*.

'Doesn't like cake?' gasped the animals.

'Allen's right,' said Mickey Thompson. 'He doesn't.'

'I'll tell you what,' said Purvis. 'Let's make some signs and arrows saying "THIS WAY MR BULLERTON", and stick them up, and by the time we've done that we might have thought of something else. OK?'

'OK!' said the others.

So Maud wrote:

"THIS WAY MISTER BULLERTON"

on a lot of pieces of paper,
Mickey Thompson and Purvis
drew a lot of arrows

on a lot of other pieces of paper,
and everyone else coloured
them blue.

'There,' said Purvis, putting
the finishing touches to the last
arrow. 'I think we're ready.'

'We're not,' said Mickey
Thompson. 'We haven't made
any plans about how to find
Raspberry.'

'RASPBERRY!' **shouted** everyone else.

'**TOOT!**' trumpeted Ortud.

'**TOOOOOOOOOOT!**'

'AH-HA,' **boomed** Maud.

'Good thinking, Ortrud.'

'Eh?' said Purvis.

'Kitchen cupboard,' said Maud.

'Sorry?' said Purvis.

'You'll see,' said Maud, as Ortrud cantered off to the small kitchen area and cr_ash^ed about and cantered back again, waving something in her trunk.

'That'll do it,' said Maud, 'it's the—'

'STRAWBERRY SAUCE!' shouted Mickey Thompson.

Raspberry

Recovery

Part 2

'**B**RILLIANT!' **shouted**
Purvis, leaping up and racing
off. 'LET'S GO!'

Allen and Ortrud and Mickey
Thompson and Maud and Peg and
Bob and Jan and Chrysanthemum

raced across the room after him,
leaping over beanbags,
knocking over cups of tea and
narrowly missing
worried-looking
animals.

'Ooh-err,' said the porcupine. 'I got splashed.'

'Sorry,' said Purvis, as he rushed by.

'So sorry,' said Allen, as he rushed by.

'I'm all damp,' grumbled the porcupine.

'GRUMBLING?' **boomed** Maud, as she rushed by.

'Sorry, Maud,' mouthed the porcupine,

as Purvis rushed out of the door
and set off up and around the
spiral steps and through the
fence and across the grass, with
Allen and Ortrud and Mickey
Thompson and Maud and Peg
and Bob and Jan and
Chrysanthemum following close
behind.

They zigzagged across the
zoo, sticking up signs and
dangling arrows in one
direction, and d r i b b l i n g
strawberry sauce in the other
direction.

'Phoof,' **puffed** Mickey

Thompson, as they jogged
along. 'I'm thirsty.'

'Me too,' **puffed** Allen. 'I
could really do with a cup of—'

'NO!' shrieked Mickey

Thompson, and everyone
skidded to a halt.

'What is it?' **puffed** Purvis.
'HOWARD'S TEA!'
shouted Mickey Thompson.

'WE'VE FORGOTTEN IT!'

So they all charged back across the grass and down the steps and through the door and into the room.

'Here we go again,' commented the porcupine.

'Sorry,' said Purvis.

'Got it,' said Allen, finding the take-away cup of tea he'd made for Howard earlier.

'Great,' said Purvis. 'Let's go.'

'Er, er,' dithered Allen.

'What's wrong, Allen?' asked Purvis.

'I'm afraid it's gone rather cold,' said Allen.

'Oh dear,' said Purvis.

'Should I make a fresh one, do you think?' said Allen.

'Um, er,' dithered Purvis.

'He'd probably prefer it hot,' said Mickey Thompson.

'Hmm,' said Purvis.

'Although he might prefer it fast,' said Mickey Thompson.

'Hmm,' said Purvis.

'Which, then?' said Allen.

'Hot,' said Mickey Thompson.

'OK,' said Allen.

'No, fast,' said Mickey Thompson.

'Help,' said Allen.

'I can't decide what to do for the best,' said Purvis.

'DITHERING?' **boomed** Maud. 'Why doesn't your Howard get his tea from **CAFÉ MARMOSET**, like normal people? Then he can make sure it's just as he likes it.'

'He has to stay behind the bush,' explained Purvis.

'BUSH?'
boomed

Maud.

'Yes,' said the mice.

'Is he *mad*?' *whispered* Maud.

'No,' said the mice.

'He sounds a little bit mad,' said Maud.

'He's not the only one,' muttered the porcupine.

'I think he sounds *lovely*,' said Chrysanthemum.

'MAD,' **boomed** Maud.

'Steady, Maud,' said

Chrysanthemum.

'STEADY, Maud,' said Maud.

'Oh, boy,' said the porcupine.

'Well, anyway,' said Purvis. 'I think we'd better get going. He can make do with cold tea for

now and we'll find him a hotter
one later.'

'Good idea,' said Allen. 'That
way he'll get two cups!'

'Yes, that's what I thought,'
said Purvis, 'and…'
'LET'S GET ON
WITH IT,' **boomed**
Maud.

'Sorry, Mau— whoops,' said Purvis.

'What?' said Maud.

'QUICK!' shouted Purvis, racing away out of the door and up the steps and through the hole and across the grass. Mickey Thompson and Maud and Peg and Bob and Jan and Ortrud and Chrysanthemum RACED off after him, and Allen followed behind a little more SLOWLY, carefully carrying Howard's cup of tea.

They hurried across the
ornamental bridge, quacked at
the ducks on the boating lake,
and passed through the Azure
Zone near the bats and
macaques, dangling arrows and
d r i b b l i n g sauce all the
way.

Finally they arrived at Howard's bush, where Howard was curled up underneath his mackintosh, snoring heavily.

'Howard,' **puffed** Purvis, prodding him.

'Wuh?' mumbled Howard.
'HOWARD,' said
Purvis, prodding
harder.

'WAAAH!'

yelled Howard,
shooting upright.
'Where am I? What's going on?'
'You're behind the bush,' said
Purvis. 'And we're back.'
'WHERE HAVE YOU
BEEN?' said Howard.
'Well,' began Purvis, 'we…'

'You've been gone AGES,' said Howard.

'I know,' said Purvis, 'we—'

'I told you NOT TO TAKE TOO LONG,' said Howard. '"*Don't take too long,*" I said.'

'Yes,' said Purvis, 'but you see…'

'"*I can't hide here all day*," I said. "*We'll be as quick as we can,*" you said,' said Howard, crossly.

'Sorry, Howard,' said Purvis. 'We got held up.'

'Hang on a minute,' spluttered Howard, suddenly noticing the other animals

hovering nearby. 'Who're all this lot?'

'Maud, Peg, Bob, Jan, and Chrysanthemum,' said Mickey Thompson.

'Helloooo,' said Maud, Peg, Bob, Jan, and Chrysanthemum, to Howard.

'I'm afraid he won't be able to understand you,' *whispered* Purvis.

'WHY?' **boomed** Maud, and Howard jumped.

'We're not sure,' said Purvis. 'It seems he can only

understand Mickey Thompson
and me.'

'So I was right,' said Maud.
'He is mad. MAD,' she
boomed, running
around in a circle. 'MAD.'

'Hush, Ortrud,' said
Howard, holding his head. 'I
can't hear myself
THINK.'

'That isn't Ortrud,' said
Mickey Thompson. 'It's Maud.'

'What are you on about?'
said Howard. 'Of course it's
Ortrud.'

'Maud,' said Mickey
Thompson.

'Ortrud,' said Howard.

'Maudtrud,' said Mickey
Thompson.

'*What?*' said Howard.

'Wait!' **gasped** Purvis,

looking around. 'Where IS
Ortrud?'

'Looking for
RASPBERRY,'
boomed Maud.

'What is wrong with you all?'
said Howard. 'And what's
wrong with her VOICE?'

'MAD,'
boomed
Maud still circling.

'MMM
MMMM
MMAD.'

'And what are all these bits of paper,' said Howard, 'and all this ... eugh,' he said, putting his hand in some sauce.

'We've been busy while you slept,' said Purvis.

'That's it!' said Howard, glazing over. 'I am asleep, and this is but a dream, and OUCH!' he squawked, as Mickey Thompson tweaked him.

'Bother,' said Howard. 'But whatever were you thinking of, Purvis? I asked for a cup of tea, not a pack of animals.'

'Ooh, I nearly forgot,' said Purvis. 'Here comes the tea now.'

'Here what the what, what?' said Howard, confusedly, as

Allen trotted around the side of the bush with the take-away cup of tea.

Howard made a gurgling noise, and fainted.

'He's fainted,' observed Mickey Thompson.

'Oh dear,' said Purvis.

'I knew I should have made a fresh one,' said Allen.

Everyone gathered round Howard and stared down at him.

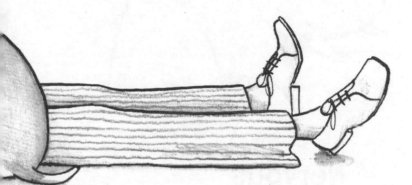

'EXPLANATION?'
boomed Maud.

'**Nervous Exhaustion**,' said Mickey Thompson.

'There's a lot of it about,' explained Purvis.

'Poor thing,' sighed
Chrysanthemum.

'What shall we do now then?'
asked Mickey Thompson,
brightly.

'I'm thinking,' said Purvis.

'Can we go and see the
unicorns?' asked Mickey
Thompson.

'Eh?' said Purvis. 'No.'

'Well, how about an ice
cream?' suggested Mickey
Thompson.

'The kiosk's been crossed out,
remember?' said Purvis. 'And
anyway, there isn't time. We've

still got to find Raspberry,
and—'

'Um,' said Allen.

'—lose Mr Bullerton, and
find Ortrud, and—'

'Excuse me,' said Allen.

'—get Howard a fresh cup of
tea, and—'

'HOY,' shouted Allen,
and everyone jumped.

'That's the way to do it,
Allen,' said Maud, approvingly.

'Yes, er, but… *ooooooh*,'
said Allen, hoPPi_{ng}, and flaPPi_{ng}
a paw.

'What is it, Allen?' asked
Purvis.

'Help!' said Allen, pointing.
'Look over there.'

Everyone peeped out over the
bush.

Everyone peered at where
Allen was pointing.

Everyone **shouted**
'EEEEEEEEK!!!!'

'What is it?' groaned
Howard, coming to.

'Wake up,' said Purvis,
prodding.

'Where am I? What's going
on?' said Howard.

'You're still behind the bush,'
whispered Purvis.

'And so will Mr Bullerton be
in about half a minute,' *whispered*
Mickey Thompson.

'YIKES!' squawked
Howard, leaping up.

'*Stay down*,' *whispered* Purvis.

'Too late,' *whispered* Mickey
Thompson, peeping out again.
'He heard.'

'What's he doing now?'
whispered Purvis.

'He's stopped,' *whispered*
Mickey Thompson.

'That's good,' *whispered* Purvis.

'He's started,' *whispered*
Mickey Thompson.

'That's bad,' *whispered* Purvis.

'He's coming,' *whispered*
Mickey Thompson.

'Oh no,' gulped Purvis.

'He's here,' squeaked Mickey
Thompson, and he and Purvis

and Maud and Peg and Bob and
Jan and Chrysanthemum and
Allen dived under Howard's
mac just in time as a shadow
loomed over the bush and Mr
Bullerton arrived, brandishing
one of the paper arrows.

Breathing heavily, Mr
Bullerton peered over the top of
the bush and stared down at
Howard, cowering behind it.

'IT'S YOU,'

thundered Mr Bullerton.

'No, it isn't,' said Howard.

'Who are you then?' demanded Mr Bullerton.

'Someone else,' said Howard.

'No, you are not,' said Mr Bullerton. 'You are Howard Armitage, and you're supposed to be working hard at your desk, NOT VISITING ZOOS.'

'That proves it then,' said Howard.

'What does?' said Mr Bullerton.

'I can't be who you think I am,' said Howard, 'because if I was I wouldn't be here, would I?'

'Eh?' said Mr Bullerton.

'Exactly,' said Howard. 'Now, it's been pleasant chatting to you, but if you'll excuse me I really must be getting on.'

'Oh, must you,' said Mr Bullerton, through **gritted** teeth.

'Indeed I must,' said Howard.

'Go on then,' said Mr Bullerton, staying put. 'Off you go.'

'Yes, well, er, right then,' said Howard, also staying put.

'What are you waiting for?' said Mr Bullerton. 'And what have you got hidden under that mac?'

'Mac?' said Howard, gazing around. 'What mac?'

'THAT GREAT SCRUFFY LUMPY ONE THERE,' **shouted** Mr Bullerton, pointing. 'You've stuffed something in it.'

'No, no,' said Howard.

'Hoh, yes,' said Mr Bullerton.

'Look, there's a tail sticking out,
and— hang on a minute, I've
seen that tail before.'

'Impossible,' said Howard.

'That tail,' said Mr Bullerton,
'belongs to the dog that belongs
to—'

'RUN!' shouted Howard, starting to run. 'HOWARD ARMITAGE!!' shouted Mr Bullerton, also starting to run.

Allen and Chrysanthemum and Jan and Bob and Peg and Maud and Purvis and Mickey Thompson shot out from under the mac and also started running.

'YOU COME BACK HERE,' shouted Mr Bullerton, chasing

Howard over the grass and
through the puddles and along
the paths, with Allen and
Chrysanthemum and Purvis and
Peg and Jan and Mickey
Thompson and Bob and Maud
chasing behind.

'GO AWAY, YOU HORRIBLE LOT,' Mr Bullerton **shouted** at them. 'SHOO!'

They carried on chasing. 'CLEAR OFF,' **shouted** Mr Bullerton.

'LEAVE ME ALONE, OR I'LL HAVE YOU LOCKED UP. ESPECIALLY THAT THING,' he **shouted**, pointing at Chrysanthemum.

Everyone chased him harder, over the ornamental bridge, twice around the boating lake and back over the bridge in the other direction.

'Why are we running?' asked a duck, joining in.

'We're chasing Mr Bullerton,' **puffed** Purvis.

'Jolly good,' said the duck,

and several of his friends joined
in too.

'THIS ZOO'S A
DISGRACE,' yelled Mr
Bullerton, sprinting off towards
the little wooden hut marked
INFORMATION POINT. 'I
SHALL HAVE IT
SHUT DOWN.'
Everyone sprinted after him
and chased him around and
around and around the little hut.

'LET ME IN,' **shouted** Mr Bullerton, **thumping** the door each time he passed it.

'**GET LOST,**' **shouted** the woman inside, each time he **thumped** it.

'LET ME IN,' **thumped** Mr Bullerton.

'**GET LOST,**' **shouted** the woman.

'LET ME IN,' **thumped** Mr Bullerton.

'**GET LOST,**' **shouted** the woman.

'I'm getting a little bit *dizzy*,' **puffed** Allen, as they

circled the hut for the
seventeenth time.

'Me too,' **puffed** Purvis.

'Oh, how can we make it stop?'
groaned Mickey Thompson.

Just then, there was a loud
too**T** and Ortrud galloped up,
waving the squeezy
bottle of strawberry sauce.
'LOOK OUT!'
shouted Purvis, and everyone
ducked as Ortrud squirted, and
Mr Bullerton skidded and
crashed, stickily, to the ground.
The door of the hut flew open
and a giraffe tottered out.

'You,'

SNARLED Mr Bullerton, nastily.

blew Raspberry, wetly, and

started to lick.

'EUGH! Stopitgetoff,'

spluttered Mr Bullerton,

struggling up.

'HOW DARE YOU!' he

thundered. 'YOU DO THAT
ONCE MORE AND I
SHALL LEAVE THIS ZOO
AND NEVER COME
BACK, AND THEN WHERE
WILL YOU ALL BE? EH?'

'*TTHPFT!*' went
Raspberry, again.

'*TTTHHPPPFFFT!!!*'

Mr Bullerton turned puce,
stomped away across the zoo
and slammed out of the big
green gate, with Raspberry and
the other zoo animals following
at a safe distance, just to make
sure.

'**Phew,**' said Purvis.

'**Toot**,' agreed Ortrud.
'What now then?' asked
Mickey Thompson.
'**CAFÉ MARMOSET**, of
course,' said Howard, patting
Allen's head. 'And the *faster* we
get there the better.'

So as *fast* as they could, they
did.

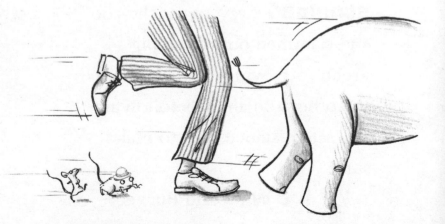